PUFFIN BOOKS

Anne Fine was born and educated in the Midlands, and now lives in County Durham. She has written numerous highly acclaimed and prize-winning books for children and adults.

Her novel *Goggle-Eyes* won the *Guardian* Children's Fiction Award and the Carnegie Medal, and was adapted for television by the BBC. *Flour Babies* won the Carnegie Medal and the Whitbread Children's Novel award. *Bill's New Frock* won a Smarties Award, *Madame Doubtfire* has become a major feature film by Twentieth Century Fox starring Robin Williams, and, most recently, *The Tulip Touch* was the winner of the Whitbread Children's Book of the Year Award for 1996.

Some other books by Anne Fine

Books for Younger Readers

Stranger Danger?
Only a Show
Scaredy-Cat
Design-a-Pram
The Worst Child I Ever Had
The Same Old Story Every Year
The Haunting of Pip Parker
The Diary of a Killer Cat

Books for Middle Range Readers

Bill's New Frock
The Country Pancake
A Sudden Puff of Glittering Smoke
A Sudden Swirl of Icy Wind
A Sudden Glow of Gold
Anneli the Art Hater
Crummy Mummy and Me
A Pack of Liars
The Angel of Nitshill Road
The Chicken Gave it to Me

ANNE FINE

Jennifer's Diary

Illustrated by Kate Aldous

PUFFIN BOOKS

PUFFIN BOOKS

Published by the Penguin Group
Penguin Books Ltd, 27 Wrights Lane, London W8 5TZ, England
Penguin Putnam Inc., 375 Hudson Street, New York, New York 10014, USA
Penguin Books Australia Ltd, Ringwood, Victoria, Australia
Penguin Books Canada Ltd, 10 Alcorn Avenue, Toronto, Ontario, Canada M4V 3B2
Penguin Books (NZ) Ltd, Private Bag 102902, NSMC, Auckland, New Zealand

On the worldwide web at: www.penguin.com

Penguin Books Ltd, Registered Offices: Harmondsworth, Middlesex, England

First published by Hamish Hamilton Ltd 1996
Published in Puffin Books 1997
Published in this edition 1999
1 3 5 7 9 10 8 6 4 2

Text copyright © Anne Fine, 1996
Illustrations copyright © Kate Aldous, 1996
All rights reserved

The moral right of the author and illustrator has been asserted

Filmset in Baskerville

Made and printed in England by Clays Ltd, St Ives plc

British Library Cataloguing in Publication Data
A CIP catalogue record for this book is available from the British Library

ISBN 0-141-30534-7

Chapter One

"IOLANTHE."

"What?"

"What are you doing?"

"I'm writing, aren't I? You can see I am. Here's the paper in front of me. This is the pen in my hand."

Jennifer sighed.

"I *know* you're writing, Iolanthe. I just want to know *what* you're writing."

"Why?"

"Because it might give me an idea."

That's the trouble with Jennifer. No ideas. Two legs, two arms, a pretty

1

face – but no imagination. None at all.

"I'm writing a story about a sheep called Hector who's suddenly realized he's going to be eaten."

2

Jennifer peered over my shoulder, and read aloud.

And so I lay forlornly in my sheep pen, reflecting on the sad fate of all who had lain there before me.

"That's very good."

"Yes," I said. "That's why I want to get on with it."

She sighed again.

"I can't think of anything to write."

She never can.

"I haven't even *started*."

Surprise, surprise.

"You think of something for me."

"Jenni*fer*!"

She shut up for a bit. I carried on, through Hector's desperate dawn escape, his daring capture of the farmer and his wife, the barbecue, and then the visit from the farm inspector.

3

"And how are Mr and Mrs Crool?"

"Excellent," said Hector. "Very, very tasty. I think the ducklings got the sauce just right."

Now Jennifer was leaning over my arm again.

"Have the animals *eaten* them?"

"Yes. Of course."

She seemed amazed.

"How did you think of *that*?"

"I just did."

"I don't know how you do it," she said crossly. "Miss Hardie says 'Write a story' and I sit here and can't think of a single word to write. You just pick up your pen and out it pours. Sensitive sheep. Cruel farmers. Cannibal cows. And I can't think of *anything*. It's not *fair*."

There must be *something* between Jennifer's ears. She can do maths, and learn poems, and even play the piano.

4

But every time I hear that old wail of hers ("I can't think of anything to write"), I want to tape her mouth shut. Or fine her fifty pence. Or move, and sit by Sarah. Or complain to Miss Hardie. Or change schools. Or slice off the top of Jennifer's head, and fill her brain up to overflowing with some of my leftover ideas.

I have too many of them. That's my trouble.

Chapter Two

WHEN WE WERE getting ready to go
home, I found a rainbow-coloured
book on the floor. I picked it up and
asked Jennifer, "Did this fall out of
your pocket?"

She put her hand out for it.

"Oh, thank you, Iolanthe."

I turned the pretty book over.

"What is it? Is it new?"

"It's a present," she said. "A diary.
From my Aunt Muriel. Every single
day of the year has a whole glossy
blank page to itself, so you can write
in it."

7

"And what have you put in it so far?"

"Nothing much," she admitted.

I opened it at the first page.

Jan 1st. It was quite cold today.

I turned the page. January 2nd was still blank. And so was January 3rd. But on January 4th, she'd spilled out all her secrets.

Mum and I went to the shops.

"So what did you buy," I asked her, "on January 4th?"

She stared at me.

"I can't remember."

"You should have put it in the diary," I said. "That's what it's for."

She snatched it back.

"You know I'm no good at writing."

"That's ideas for Miss Hardie,"

I said. "But this is a diary. You didn't have to make things up. You could have just written down what happened."

"Not much did."

"Then you could have written something else in it," I said. "Like Inner Thoughts."

She looked as blank as January 2nd.

"Inner Thoughts?"

"You know," I said. "Things like Unspoken Fears. Private Worries. Secret Hopes. Everyone has those."

Jennifer gave me a funny look, as if to say, 'Maybe *you* do, Iolanthe. But *I* don't.' Then she went off, to walk home with Sarah. I go the other way. So when I saw the diary on the ground again, just outside school, instead of chasing after the two of them to give it back, I picked it up and took it home with me.

Diaries are deeply private. I know that.

So it sat on the table while I was having tea, and I didn't even touch it.

It sat on the arm of the sofa while I

was watching telly. I didn't even peep inside.

And it sat on the laundry basket while I was having my bath. I didn't even nose through the pages, looking for good bits I'd missed.

I didn't crack until bedtime. Then I read all the bits I'd read before, while Jennifer was watching. (*Jan 1st. It was quite cold today.* Blank. Blank. *Jan 4th. Mum and I went to the shops.*) The next two pages were just two more blanks. Then:

Jan 7th. Nothing much happened.

And that was that.

I'm serious. I turned over every page, and there was no more. Not a single word. And it's the eleventh today.

Sad life.

Chapter Three

I ONLY WROTE in it because it was there. I wasn't being spiteful. It's just that I was tucked up in my bed, not at all tired, with nothing else to do. My pen was practically *waving* at me out of my school bag. And the next page in the diary was so smooth and white and empty, it seemed to be *begging* for help.

"Help! Help!"
The words still ring in my ears.
"Help! Help!"
Today (January 11th) *I saved a little*

boy's life. I'm not that brave. In fact Iolanthe, who sits next to me in class, often says I'm a wimp. But when I saw that poor child drowning in the river on the way to school, I didn't stop to think. I just tore off my clothes, and jumped, in my knickers, into the freezing water.

The boy was panicking.

"Stop struggling," I warned. "Or I'll have to knock you out."

He kept on thrashing, so I bopped him,
hard. His eyes rolled horribly, but he was no
more trouble. So slowly, slowly I hauled him
back to the bank, and dragged him out.

A woman flew out of the bushes.

"My son!" she cried. "My own dear son!
How cold and wet you are!"

She scooped him up, and ran off towards a

little house some way along the river.

I wondered whether to go after her. But then the school bell rang.

Five to nine!

Quickly, I pulled on my clothes and ran. My knickers are still wet. But otherwise I'm fine. Just happy to have saved a life. And happy I wasn't late.

Good story, I thought. And it just fitted neatly on the page. So how was I to know it was going to cause so much trouble? How was I to know Miss Hardie would look round the classroom the very next morning, and then pick on Jennifer?

"Remember those stories I asked you all to write yesterday? Jennifer, why don't you read us yours?"

Jennifer looked anxious.

"I didn't really get started," she admitted.

Miss Hardie looked so cross that I thought I'd better come to Jennifer's rescue.

"She was too busy writing in her diary," I explained.

"Right, then," Miss Hardie said cheerfully. "Why don't you read us some of that instead?"

Jennifer picked it up, and flicked through the first few pages.

"There isn't really much in it."

Miss Hardie was getting cross again now.

"Well, read it anyway," she snapped.

So Jennifer began to read.

"Jan 1st. It was quite cold today. Jan 4th. Mum and I went to the shops."

Her voice trailed off. She turned the next few pages rather hopelessly, waiting for Miss Hardie's explosion.

And then, suddenly, like manna from heaven, she came across my bit.

"Help! Help!"
The words still ring in my ears.

I thought she read the story out rather well, considering it came as such a surprise. I couldn't understand

why she got so ratty after. Everyone was crowding round her, telling her how *brave* she was, and how *exciting* it must have been, and how *rude* the boy's mother was not to come back and say thank you to the person who had just saved her poor son from a watery grave.

And all Jennifer could do was hiss at me tearfully:

"How *could* you, Iolanthe! Wet knickers! I've never had wet knickers in my life!"

Chapter Four

WE MADE UP later that morning. We had to, because Miss Hardie got so fed up with the noise, she made everybody in the class settle down and write a story called *Time Travel*.

Jennifer was stuck, and I needed to borrow her second-best ballpoint.

"I'll only lend it to you if you share your idea with me."

"I'll only share my idea with you if you stop being mad at me."

"All right."

"All right."

So I shared my idea with her. It was
brilliant.

"Pretend we have to come back to
school in fifty years' time, for Open
Day. Just write down what you think
this place will be like by the time you
and I are about sixty."

She stared at me admiringly.

"You're so *clever*, Iolanthe."

"Yes, I am," I said. But she didn't
look shocked, like she usually does

when I say that, because she'd already
started. I read it over her shoulder. It
was really dull. All about how much
taller the trees had grown, and how
the entrance hall was painted blue
now, not green. And how all the pupils
had tiny computers built into their
desks, and the teachers took them on
rocket trips to the moon instead of
bus rides to the museum.

"Stop reading over my shoulder,"

she complained. "Get on with your own work."

So I did.

It hardly seems over half a century since I was last here, I wrote. *Personally, I still feel, and look, like the vibrant and beautiful young girl I was then. But the rust on the old school gates is something shocking. And, golly, there's been some litter dropped in sixty years. I had to wade through lolly wrappers to reach the front door.*

And what a shock greeted me there!

Miss Hardie (far too old to teach, poor dear) almost fell off her zimmer frame trying to open the door to me. Her hair was snowy-white. The veins on her hands looked like tree roots. Her ill-fitting false teeth clacked horribly as she spoke.

"Who is it?"

She peered at me blindly. Then:

"Is it –? Can it be – ? Yes!" she cried in her

cracked and quavering old voice. "It's Iolanthe Jones! Come in, my dear! How lovely to see you! You were always my favourite pupil."

I smiled my usual modest smile as Miss Hardie's lined face suddenly became even more wrinkled.

"Now, who was that little girl who used to sit next to you, Iolanthe? That poor, pathetic creature who could never think of any –

Sensing danger, I looked up. Jennifer was watching me very closely indeed.

– *names for her pet kittens*, I wrote hastily.

I thought I'd be safe with that. (Jennifer's allergic to fur.) But, no. She went straight into a giant sulk.

"You're *horrible*, Iolanthe," she said. "You're so mean that I'm phoning my mum to tell her not to bother to come and pick me up at lunchtime. Because I won't need to go shopping for a new

frock, because I'm not coming to your party."

"You can't phone her. The phone's broken. And I wasn't being mean. I wasn't writing about you. I was writing about a person I haven't even sat by yet. That's what Time Travel's all about."

I don't know if she believed me. I know she didn't try to phone. But, then again, I didn't really expect her to, because if there's one thing that Jennifer absolutely loves, it's a party. Even one of mine.

Chapter Five

IT WAS HER own fault for getting back so late. If she'd been here, I'd have been able to do the same as everyone else, and work in a pair. But since I was a leftover, Miss Hardie said firmly, "Do something useful while you're waiting, Iolanthe."

So I wrote in the diary. I wrote in the diary because no one else was using it. All Jennifer had written was:
Jan 13th. The sky's a bit pink today.

I started on January 14th.

"No! Not pink! Never pink!"

29

"Please, Mother," I begged. "Oh, let me buy a pink frock to go to Iolanthe's party."

My mother shrieked in horror.

"No! Never pink! Not after what happened to your Great Aunt Lucy."

"What happened to Great Aunt Lucy?"

"It's too terrible to tell."

I begged. I pleaded. I even wept. And, finally, my mother told me.

"Your Great Aunt Lucy knew that we had a ghost. Dozens of people had seen The Child In Pink. She floated in and out of walls, and groaned at midnight, and on the stormiest nights her sobs were heard in the nursery. Everyone knew her story. She was a disobedient child. Her mother had told her a hundred times: 'Stay away from the nasty dark cellars.' But would she listen? No! She wandered in and out, and one day, she got lost and disappeared."

"What did they do?"

"They searched, of course. High and low,

31

calling her name. But by the time they found her, she was dead. Quite dead!"

"Quite dead?"

"Well, not quite dead, because from that day on, she haunted them. In and out of walls. Groaning and sobbing. Until the day your Great Aunt Lucy wore pink to go to a party. Lucy put on her frock, and then, with half an hour to spare, she wandered off, down to the cellars."

"No!"

"Yes! And just like The Child In Pink, she wandered in and out of cold dark places. Some say she saw a child her own age, beckoning. And others say she heard a sweet little voice. "Don't go to that party. Come to mine!" All that we know is that your Great Aunt Lucy was never seen alive again. And now, on stormy nights, instead of sobbing, we hear peals of laughter. At midnight, instead of *groans, we hear two sweet voices singing. And instead of seeing one child in pink float through the walls, people see two, hand in hand. And people say –*

Jennifer came rushing back in then, all red-faced, holding a great big carrier bag.

"You're terribly late," Miss Hardie scolded her. "The bell rang a long time ago."

"Mum says she's sorry and it will never happen again," Jennifer panted. "It's just that I had to get a frock for Iolanthe's party. The traffic both ways was frightful. And it took us forever to find something the right colour."

She fell in her seat, still panting.

"Which colour's that, then?" I asked.

"Pink," Jennifer said proudly.

Just as proudly, I pointed to the first line of my story.

"No! Not pink! Never pink!"

Jennifer snatched her diary and read through what I'd written. She was so cross again, she wouldn't speak to me the whole afternoon. And I think she

only came to my party because her
mother made her.

   She wore blue.

Chapter Six

I WANTED THE diary so much.

"Please!" I begged Jennifer. "It's wasted on someone like you. You hardly use it. *Please* give it to me."

"What will you give me for it?"

I lifted up my desk lid.

"Nothing," I said sadly. "There's nothing in here anyone would want."

Jennifer shrugged.

"I'll just keep it for now, then."

"But you don't write anything in it!"

"That's because nothing happens."

"No, it's not."

She let me fill in the empty pages,

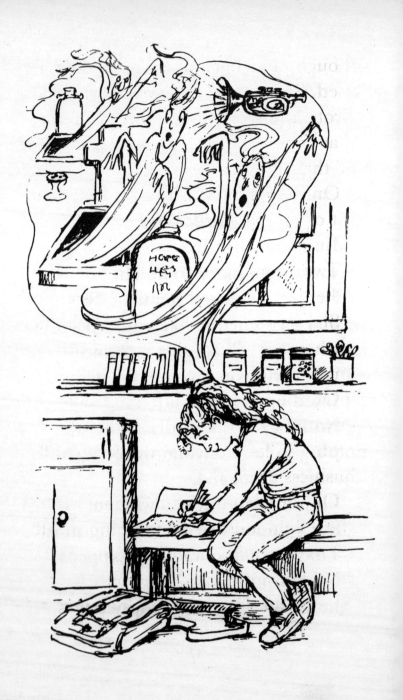

though. The back ones she hadn't used. So on the January 2nd page, I wrote a horror story about a trumpet that could call freshly dead people out of their graves.

On the January 3rd page, I made a list of all my Unspoken Fears, in code. (Mind your own business.)

Two pages later, I wrote a poem called *Stamping on Granny's Daisies*.

She wanted it back then, so I let her have it. But she couldn't think of anything to write.

On the January 6th page, I put down my Private Worries in strict alphabetical order. (Mind your own business again.)

On the blank page of January 8th, I started on a list of Secret Hopes. But there was only one. (That Jennifer would give me the diary.) So I gave up, and started another ghost tale.

And it was as well I hadn't used up the space, because the story got so complicated, it went on through blank pages January 9th and 10th. And even then I had to finish it in tiny writing, so as not to get tangled in *"Help! Help!"* on the 11th.

On the January 12th page, I wrote a letter begging for the diary.

Dear, sweet and lovely Jennifer,

All of my life, I have longed for a diary like this one to write all my ideas and thoughts in. It's kind of you to lend it when I ask. But borrowing's not like having. This diary and I were made for one another. We shouldn't be parted for a single hour.

And I kept on, for the whole page, with Jennifer pretending she wasn't reading it over my shoulder.

"What now?" I asked her. "I've run out of room until tomorrow."

"Maybe I'll use up tomorrow's page myself."

"I doubt it."

"I *might*," she snapped.

I didn't want to argue. (I was still hoping she would give it to me.) So I went back and filled in all her old half-used days.

I stared at her January 1st (*It was quite cold today.*) and then picked up my pen.

But not cold enough to stop noble and kind Iolanthe taking soup to the poor. From my window, I watched her pick her way over snow and ice to old Mrs Morris's hovel. Inside that rude hut lie sixteen shivering children, all half-starved. If it weren't for dear Iolanthe –

Miss Hardie interrupted me in mid-flow.

"Iolanthe! Come up to my desk, please. I want a little word with you."

You couldn't really call what she had with me 'a little word'. It was more like a giant great lecture, all

about 'pushing my luck', and 'going too far', and 'the point at which imagination shades into simple rudeness'.

I had to say sorry about a million times, and then stick clean white paper over most of my Time Travel story and write in something else over the top. It took a lot of time, so it wasn't till the next day that I got round to filling in Jennifer's mostly-empty January 4th (*Mum and I went to the shops.*)

Mum and I went to the shops.

"Quick!" she said. "Stuff this up your pinny, Jennifer, and I'll hide this in my bag."

"Mother!" I said. "You mustn't shoplift! It's quite wrong!"

Her face cracked into an evil scowl.

"I'm not your mother!" she cried. "It's time you knew, Jennifer. There was a mix-up at the hospital when you were born. This high-born lady and myself were sharing a room. The cots lay side by side. And in the middle of the night —

I broke off. I had to. Jennifer was stabbing me with her pen.

"Stop it!" she ordered. "Stop it!"

Normally, I'd have argued. But I'd been in such trouble already that week that I just shrugged, and moved on to her January 7th. *(Nothing much happened today.)*

Nothing much happened today. After the spaceship landed and all the blobmen had blobbled down the ladder into the woods –

"Iolanthe!"

"Yes, Miss Hardie?"

"That's not your workbook you're writing in, is it?"

"No, Miss Hardie. It's Jennifer's diary."

"Give it back."

Does *no one* want me to be happy?

No one at *all*? I sulked for the rest of the day. I tried to tell myself that pretty rainbow-coloured books don't matter. It's the stories that count. But I wanted Jennifer's diary *so much*. If I could get her to give it to me, for keeps, I could start off from January 15th. That would mean three hundred and fifty pages left.

All blank and gleaming and glossy. And all mine.

What I needed was something to trade. But I had nothing Jennifer might want. My desk was full of rubbish. Most of the stuff I have at home has to be shared with my sister. And I owe pocket money for a hundred years.

But "Curly hair, curly thoughts" says my granny.

Let's hope she's right . . .

Chapter Seven

THE VERY NEXT morning, I opened Jennifer's diary to January 15th.

"Don't you start writing on today's page," she told me. "I might want to use it myself later."

See how this sharing isn't working out?

I flicked back to the last only slightly-used page.

Jan 13th. The sky's a bit pink today.

I gazed at it, chewing my pen and screwing up my face. I drummed my fingers on the desk. I rolled my eyes.

"What's the matter?" asked Jennifer.

"I can't think of anything to write,"
I told her.

Jennifer stared.

"What? *You?*"

"Yes," I said snappily. "*Me.*"

Jennifer looked anxious.

"Are you ill, Iolanthe?"

"No. I'm not ill."

"Then what's happened?"

"Nothing's happened," I told her. "It's just that I don't seem to have any ideas."

"That's strange, for you."

"Yes, isn't it?"

We stared at it together for a while.

The sky's a bit pink today.

Then Jennifer said guiltily, "Maybe it's my fault. I was the one who wrote it, after all. And it is a bit boring."

Bit boring? *The sky's a bit pink today* is START ME OFF WITH A YAWN. But I was too canny to say so.

"Not at all. And, anyhow, I ought to be able to think of *something*."

We both stared some more. I felt it was important to keep her attention, so:

"Suppose . . .?" I said hesitantly.

Then, shaking my head, "No. Forget it."

That set her off.

"What about . . .?" As usual, she stopped. "No. That's no good."

It's not my style, but I was getting in the swing of it.

"What if . . .?" I broke off. "No.

That's stupid."

Encouraged, she tried again herself.

"Could you . . .?" Sadly, she brushed the idea aside. "No. That's hopeless, too."

I turned to look at her with wide, sincere eyes.

"Jennifer," I said. "I want to tell you I'm sorry. I've been a brute. A horrid, impatient brute. I never thought about how awful it must feel to be a person who has no ideas. I promise I'll never again tease you, or get crabby when you can't think of anything to write."

Her eyes lit up.

"Really?"

"Really," I said. "In fact, I *almost* feel that if I ever had two ideas in future, and you had none, I'd give you one of mine."

She turned to look at me closely.

"You almost think that?"

"Yes, *almost*."

She picked up the diary and gazed at it thoughtfully.

"Do you think having this might just push you over?"

"Push me over?"

"From *almost* to *definitely*."

"Yes, it might." I laid a finger on it and shut my eyes. "In fact, I have a feeling it might even help me get my ideas back."

She shoved it into my hand.

"Here. Take it. It's yours."

"Really? For keeps?"

"For keeps."

I held it tightly, and stared into space.

"I think it's working," I said hopefully. "Yes. Yes! I believe it's working. In fact, at this very moment, I feel an idea welling up."

"*Two*," Jennifer said firmly.

"Yes. *Two* ideas," I agreed hastily. "One for me, one for you."

"That's better," she said tartly.

I'm keeping hers, of course, until she needs it. I've started off on mine.

The sky's a bit pink today. Ever since Venus exploded, and shattered Mars, the colours have been startling. The few of us who weren't blinded by the flashes sit by the fire –

And it's a good idea. But pretending I'd run out of ideas was even better.

I can't write that one in the diary, though.

Jennifer might see.

ANNE FINE

The Diary of
a Killer Cat

Illustrated by Steve Cox

PUFFIN BOOKS

PUFFIN BOOKS

Published by the Penguin Group
Penguin Books Ltd, 27 Wrights Lane, London W8 5TZ, England
Penguin Putnam Inc., 375 Hudson Street, New York, New York 10014, USA
Penguin Books Australia Ltd, Ringwood, Victoria, Australia
Penguin Books Canada Ltd, 10 Alcorn Avenue, Toronto, Ontario, Canada M4V 3B2
Penguin Books (NZ) Ltd, Private Bag 102902, NSMC, Auckland, New Zealand

On the worldwide web at: www.penguin.com

Penguin Books Ltd, Registered Offices: Harmondsworth, Middlesex, England

First published by Hamish Hamilton Ltd 1994
Published in Puffin Books 1996
Published in this edition 1999
1 3 5 7 9 10 8 6 4 2

Filmset in Baskerville

Made and printed in England by Clays Ltd, St Ives plc

British Library Cataloguing in Publication Data
A CIP catalogue record for this book is available from the British Library

ISBN 0–141–30534–7

1: Monday

OKAY, OKAY. So hang me. I killed the bird. For pity's sake, I'm a *cat*. It's practically my *job* to go creeping round the garden after sweet little eensy-weensy birdy-pies that can hardly fly from one hedge to another. So what am I supposed to do when one of the poor feathery little flutterballs just about throws itself into my mouth? I mean, it practically landed on my paws. It could have *hurt* me.

   Okay, *okay*. So I biffed it. Is that any reason for Ellie to cry in my fur so hard I almost *drown*, and squeeze me so hard I almost *choke*?

"Oh, Tuffy!" she says, all sniffles and red eyes and piles of wet tissues. "Oh, Tuffy. How could you *do* that?"

How could I *do* that? I'm a *cat*. How did I know there was going to be such a giant great fuss, with Ellie's mother rushing off to fetch sheets of old

Oh Tuffy!

newspaper, and Ellie's father filling a
bucket with soapy water?

Okay, *okay*. So maybe I shouldn't
have dragged it in and left it on the
carpet. And maybe the stains won't
come out, ever.

So *hang* me.

2: *Tuesday*

I QUITE ENJOYED the little funeral. I
don't think they really wanted me to
come, but, after all, it's just as much
my garden as theirs. In fact, I spend a
whole lot more time in it than they do.
I'm the only one in the family who
uses it properly.

Not that they're grateful. You ought
to hear them.

"That cat is *ruining* my flower beds.
There are hardly any of the petunias
left."

"I'd barely *planted* the lobelias before
it was lying on top of them, squashing

them flat."

"I *do* wish it wouldn't dig holes in the anemones."

Moan, moan, moan, moan. I don't know why they bother to keep a cat, since all they ever seem to do is complain.

All except Ellie. She was too busy being soppy about the bird. She put it in a box, and packed it round with cotton wool, and dug a little hole, and then we all stood round it while she said a few words, wishing the bird luck in heaven.

"Go away," Ellie's father hissed at me. (I find that man quite rude.) But I just flicked my tail at him. Gave him the blink. Who does he think he is? If I want to watch a little birdy's funeral, I'll watch it. After all, I've known the bird longer than any of them have. I knew it when it was *alive*.

3: Wednesday

SO SPANK ME! I brought a dead mouse into their precious house. I didn't even kill it. When I came across it, it was already a goner. Nobody's safe around here. This avenue is ankle-deep in rat poison, fast cars charge up and down at all hours, and I'm not the only cat around here. I don't even know what happened to the thing. All I know is, I found it. It was already dead. (Fresh dead, but dead.) And at the time I thought it was a good idea to bring it home. Don't ask me why. I must have been crazy. How did I know that Ellie

7

was going to grab me and give me one of her little talks?

"Oh, Tuffy! That's the second time this week. I can't bear it. I know you're a cat, and it's natural and everything. But please, for my sake, stop."

She gazed into my eyes.

"Will you stop? Please?"

I gave her the blink. (Well, I tried. But she wasn't having any.)

"I *mean* it, Tuffy," she told me. "I love you, and I understand how you feel. But you've got to stop doing this, okay?"

She had me by the paws. What could I say? So I tried to look all sorry. And then she burst into tears all over again, and we had another funeral.

This place is turning into Fun City. It really is.

8

4: *Thursday*

OKAY, OKAY! I'll try and explain about
the rabbit. For starters, I don't think
anyone's given me enough credit for
getting it through the cat-flap. That
was *not easy*. I can tell you, it took
about an hour to get that rabbit
through that little hole. That rabbit
was downright *fat*. It was more like a
pig than a rabbit, if you want my
opinion.

Not that any of them cared what I
thought. They were going mental.

"It's Thumper!" cried Ellie. "It's
next-door's Thumper!"

10

"Oh, Lordy!" said Ellie's father. "Now we're in trouble. What are we going to do?"

Ellie's mother stared at me.

"How could a cat *do* that?" she asked. "I mean, it's not like a tiny bird, or a mouse, or anything. That rabbit is the same size as Tuffy. They both weigh a *ton*."

Nice. Very nice. This is my *family*, I'll have you know. Well, Ellie's family. But you take my point.

And Ellie, of course, freaked out. She went berserk.

"It's horrible," she cried. "*Horrible*. I can't believe that Tuffy could have done that. Thumper's been next door for years and years and years."

Sure. Thumper was a friend. I knew him well.

She turned on me.

11

"Tuffy! This is the end. That poor, poor rabbit. Look at him!"

And Thumper did look a bit of a mess, I admit it. I mean, most of it was only mud. And a few grass stains, I suppose. And there were quite a few bits of twig and stuff stuck in his fur. And he had a streak of oil on one ear. But no one gets dragged the whole way across a garden, and through a hedge, and over another garden, and through a freshly-oiled cat-flap, and ends up looking as if they're just off to a party.

And Thumper didn't care what he looked like. He was *dead*.

The rest of them minded, though. They minded a *lot*.

"What are we going to do?"

"Oh, this is dreadful. Next-door will never speak to us again."

"We must think of something."

13

And they did. I have to say, it was a brilliant plan, by any standards. First, Ellie's father fetched the bucket again, and filled it with warm soapy water. (He gave me a bit of a look as he did this, trying to make me feel guilty for the fact that he'd had to dip his hands in the old Fairy Liquid twice in one week. I just gave him my old 'I-am-not-impressed' stare back.)

Then Ellie's mother dunked Thumper in the bucket and gave him a nice bubbly wash and a swill-about. The water turned a pretty nasty brown colour. (All that mud.) And then, glaring at me as if it were all *my* fault, they tipped it down the sink and began over again with fresh soap suds.

Ellie was snivelling, of course.

"Do stop that, Ellie," her mother said. "It's getting on my nerves. If you

want to do something useful, go and
fetch the hairdrier."

So Ellie trailed upstairs, still bawling
her eyes out.

I sat on the top of the dresser, and
watched them.

They up-ended poor Thumper and
dunked him again in the bucket.
(Good job he wasn't his old self. He'd
have hated all this washing.) And
when the water finally ran clear, they
pulled him out and drained him.

15

Then they plonked him on newspaper, and gave Ellie the hairdrier.

"There you go," they said. "Fluff him up nicely."

Well, she got right into it, I can tell you. That Ellie could grow up to be a real hot-shot hairdresser, the way she fluffed him up. I have to say, I never saw Thumper look so nice before, and he lived in next-door's hutch for years and years, and I saw him every day.

"Hiya, Thump," I'd sort of nod at him as I strolled over the lawn to check out what was left in the feeding bowls further down the avenue.

"Hi, Tuff," he'd sort of twitch back.

Yes, we were good mates. We were pals. And so it was really nice to see him looking so spruced up and smart when Ellie had finished with him.

He looked *good*.

"What now?" said Ellie's father.

Ellie's mum gave him a look – the sort of look she sometimes gives me, only nicer.

"Oh, no," he said. "Not me. Oh, no, no, no, no, no."

"It's you or me," she said. "And I can't go, can I?"

"Why not?" he said. "You're smaller than I am. You can crawl through the hedge easier."

That's when I realised what they had in mind. But what could I say? What could I do to stop them? To *explain*?

Nothing. I'm just a cat.

I sat and watched.

5: *Friday*

I CALL IT Friday because they left it so late. The clock was already well past midnight by the time Ellie's father finally heaved himself out of his comfy chair in front of the telly and went upstairs. When he came down again he was dressed in black. Black from head to foot.

"You look like a cat burglar," said Ellie's mother.

"I wish someone would burgle *our* cat," he muttered.

I just ignored him. I thought that was best.

Together they went to the back door.

"Don't switch the outside light on," he warned her. "You never know who might be watching."

I tried to sneak out at the same time,
but Ellie's mother held me back with
her foot.

"You can just stay inside tonight,"
she told me. "We've had enough
trouble from you this week."

21

Fair's fair. And I heard all about it anyway, later, from Bella and Tiger and Pusskins. They all reported back. (They're good mates.) They all saw Ellie's father creeping across the lawn, with his plastic bag full of Thumper (wrapped nicely in a towel to keep him clean). They all saw him forcing his way through the hole in the hedge, and crawling across next-door's lawn on his tummy.

"Couldn't think *what* he was doing," Pusskins said afterwards.

"*Ruined* the hole in the hedge," complained Bella. "He's made it so big that the Thompson's rottweiler could get through it now."

"That father of Ellie's must have the most dreadful night vision," said Tiger. "It took him forever to find that hutch in the dark."

"And prise the door open."

"And stuff in poor old Thumper."

"And set him out neatly on his bed of straw."

"All curled up."

"With the straw patted up round him."

"So it looked as if he was sleeping."

"It was very, very lifelike," said Bella. "It could have fooled me. If anyone just happened to be passing in the dark, they'd really have thought that poor old Thumper had just died happily and peacefully in his sleep, after a good life, from old age."

They all began howling with laughter.

"Sshh!" I said. "Keep it down, guys. They'll hear, and I'm not supposed to be out tonight. I'm grounded."

They all stared at me.

"Get away with you!"

"Grounded?"

"What *for*?"

"Murder," I said. "For cold-blooded bunnicide."

That set us all off again. We yowled and yowled. The last I heard before we took off in a gang up Beechcroft Drive was one of the bedroom windows being flung open, and Ellie's father yelling, "How did you get out, you crafty beast?"

So what's he going to do? Nail up the cat-flap?

6: *Still Friday*

HE NAILED UP the cat-flap. Would you
believe this man? He comes down the
stairs this morning, and before he's
even out of his pyjamas he's set to
work with the hammer and a nail.

Bang, bang, bang, bang!

I'm giving him the stare, I really
am. But then he turns round and
speaks to me directly.

"There," he says. "That'll fix you.
Now it swings *this* way – " He gives
the cat-flap a hefty shove with his foot.
"But it doesn't swing *this* way."

And, sure enough, when the flap

tried to flap back in, it couldn't. It hit the nail.

"So," he says to me. "You can go out. Feel free to go out. Feel free, in fact, not only to go out, but also to stay out, get lost, or disappear for ever. But should you bother to come back again, don't go to the trouble of bringing anything with you. Because this is now a one-way flap, and so you will have to sit on the doormat until one of the family lets you in."

He narrows his eyes at me, all nasty-like.

"And woe betide you, Tuffy, if there's anything dead lying waiting on the doormat beside you."

'Woe betide you'! What a stupid expression. What on earth does it mean anyway? 'Woe betide you'!

Woe betide *him*.

7: *Saturday*

I HATE SATURDAY morning. It's so unsettling, all that fussing and door-banging and "Have you got the purse?" and "Where's the shopping list?" and "Do we need catfood?" Of course we need catfood. What else am I supposed to eat all week? Air?

They were all pretty quiet today, though. Ellie was sitting at the table carving Thumper a rather nice gravestone out of half a leftover cork floor tile. It said:

Thumper
Rest in peace

"You mustn't take it round next-door yet," her father warned her. "Not till they've told us Thumper's dead, at any rate."

Some people are born soft. Her eyes brimmed with tears.

"There goes Next-door now," Ellie's mother said, looking out of the window.

"Which way is she headed?"

"Towards the shops."

"Good. If we keep well behind, we can get Tuffy to the vet's without bumping into her."

Tuffy? Vet's?

Ellie was even more horrified than I was. She threw herself at her father, beating him with her soft little fists.

"Dad! No! You can't!"

I put up a far better fight with my claws. When he finally prised me out of the dark of the cupboard under the sink, his woolly was ruined and his hands were scratched and bleeding all over.

He wasn't very pleased about it.

"Come out of there, you great fat

35

furry psychopath. It's only a 'flu jab
you're booked in for – more's the
pity!''

Would *you* have believed him? I wasn't absolutely sure. (Neither was Ellie, so she tagged along.) I was still quite suspicious when we reached the vet's. That is *the only reason* why I spat at the girl behind the desk. There was no reason on earth to write HANDLE WITH CARE at the top of my case notes. Even the Thompson's rottweiler doesn't have HANDLE WITH CARE written on the top of his case notes. What's wrong with *me*?

So I was a little rude in the waiting room. So what? I *hate* waiting. And I especially hate waiting stuffed in a wire cat cage. It's cramped. It's hot. And it's boring. After a few hundred minutes of sitting there quietly, *anyone* would start teasing their neighbours. I didn't *mean* to frighten that little sick baby gerbil half to death. I was only *looking* at it. It's a free country, isn't it? Can't a cat even *look* at a sweet little baby gerbil?

And if I was licking my lips (which I wasn't) that's only because I was thirsty. Honestly. I wasn't trying to pretend I was going to eat it.

The trouble with baby gerbils is they can't take a *joke*.

And neither can anyone else round here.

Ellie's father looked up from the pamphlet he was reading called "*Your Pet and Worms*". (Oh, nice. Very nice.)

"Turn the cage round the other way, Ellie," he said.

Ellie turned my cage round the other way.

Now I was looking at the Fisher's terrier. (And if there's any animal in the world who ought to have HANDLE WITH CARE written at the top of his case notes, it's the Fisher's terrier).

Okay, so I hissed at him. It was only a little hiss. You practically had to have bionic ears to *hear* it.

And I did growl a bit. But you'd think he'd have a head start on growling. He is a dog, after all. I'm only a cat.

And yes, okay, I spat a bit. But only a bit. Nothing you'd even *notice* unless you were waiting to pick on someone.

Well, how was *I* to know he wasn't feeling very well? Not *everyone* waiting for the vet is ill. *I* wasn't ill, was I? Actually, I've never been ill in my life. I don't even know what it *feels* like. But I reckon, even if I were *dying*, something furry locked in a cage could make an eensy-weensy noise at me

without my ending up whimpering and cowering, and scrabbling to get under the seat, to hide behind the knees of my owner.

More a *chicken* than a Scotch terrier, if you want my opinion.

"Could you please keep that vile cat of yours under control?" Mrs Fisher said nastily.

Ellie stuck up for me.

"He is in a cage!"

"He's still scaring half the animals in here to death. Can't you cover him up, or something?"

Ellie was going to keep arguing, I could tell. But, without even looking up from his worm pamphlet, her father just dropped his raincoat over my cage as if I were some mangy old *parrot* or something.

And everything went black.

No wonder by the time the vet came at me with her nasty long needle, I was in a bit of a mood. I didn't mean to scratch her that badly, though.

Or smash all those little glass bottles.

Or tip the expensive new cat scales off the bench.

Or spill all that cleaning fluid.

It wasn't me who ripped my record card into tiny pieces, though. That was the vet.

43

When we left, Ellie was in tears again. (Some people are born soft.) She hugged my cage tightly to her chest.

"Oh, Tuffy! Until we find a new vet who'll promise to look after you, you must be so careful not to get run over."

"Fat chance!" her father muttered.

I was just glowering at him through the cage wire, when he spotted Ellie's mother, standing knee-deep in shopping bags outside the supermarket.

"You're very late," she scolded. "Was there a bit of trouble at the vet's?"

Ellie burst into tears. I mean, talk about *wimp*. But her father is made of sterner stuff. He'd just taken the most huge breath, ready to snitch on me,

when suddenly he let it out again. Out of the corner of his eye, he'd spotted trouble of another sort.

"Quick!" he whispered. "Next-door is just coming through the check-out."

He picked up half the shopping bags. Ellie's mother picked up the rest. But before we could get away, next-door had come through the glass doors.

So now all four of them were forced to chat.

"Morning," said Ellie's father.

"Morning," said Next-door.

"Nice day," said Ellie's father.

"Lovely," agreed Next-door.

"Nicer than yesterday," said Ellie's mother.

"Oh, yes," Next-door said. "Yesterday was *horrible*."

She probably just meant the

weather, for heaven's sake. But Ellie's eyes filled with tears. (I don't know why she was so fond of Thumper. *I'm* the one who's supposed to be her pet, not *him*.) And because she couldn't see where she was going properly any more, she bumped into her mother, and half the tins of catfood fell out of one of the shopping bags, and rolled off down the street.

Ellie dumped down my cage, and
chased off after them. Then she made
the mistake of reading the labels.

"Oh, nooo!" she wailed. "Rabbit
chunks!"

(Really, that child is such a *drip*.
She'd never make it in our gang. She
wouldn't last a *week*.)

"Talking about rabbit," said
Next-door. "The most extraordinary
thing happened at our house."

"Really?" said Ellie's father, glaring
at me.

"Oh, yes?" said Ellie's mother,
glaring at me as well.

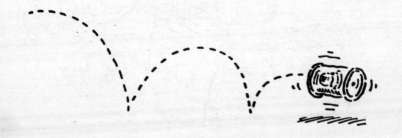

"Yes," said Next-door. "On
Monday, poor Thumper looked a little
bit poorly, so we brought him inside.
And on Tuesday, he was worse. And
on Wednesday he died. He was
terribly old, and he'd had a happy life,
so we didn't feel too bad about it. In

fact we had a little funeral, and buried him in a box at the bottom of the garden."

I'm staring up at the clouds now.

"And on Thursday, he'd gone."

"Gone?"

"Gone?"

"Yes, gone. And all there was left of him was a hole in the ground and an empty box."

"Really?"

"Good heavens!"

Ellie's father was giving me the most suspicious look.

"And then, yesterday," Next-door went on. "Something even more extraordinary happened. Thumper was back again. All fluffed up nicely, and back in his hutch."

"Back in his hutch, you say?"

"Fluffed up nicely? How strange!"

You have to hand it to them, they're good actors. They kept it up all the way home.

"What an amazing story!"

"How on earth could it have happened?"

"Quite astonishing!"

"So strange!"

Till we were safely through the front door. And then, of course, the pair of them turned on me.

"Deceitful creature!"

"Making us think you killed him!"

"Just pretending all along!"

"I *knew* that cat could never have done it. That rabbit was even fatter than he is!"

You'd have thought they all *wanted* me to have murdered old Thumper.

All except Ellie. She was *sweet*.

"Don't you *dare* pick on Tuffy!" she told them. "You leave him alone! I bet he didn't even dig poor Thumper up. I bet it was the Fisher's nasty, vicious terrier who did that. All Tuffy did was bring Thumper back to us so we could make sure he was buried again properly. He's a hero. A kind and thoughtful hero."

She gave me a big soft squeeze.

"Isn't that right, Tuffy?"

I'm saying nothing, am I? I'm a cat.
So I just sat and watched while they
unnailed the cat-flap.

Flour Babies

by Anne Fine

When the annual school science fair comes round, Mr Cartwright's class don't get to work on the Soap Factory, the Maggot Farm or the Exploding Custard Tins. To their intense disgust they get the Flour Babies – sweet little six-pound bags of flour that must be cared for at all times.

Young Simon Martin, a committed hooligan, approaches the task with little enthusiasm. But as the days pass, he not only grows fond of his flour baby, he also comes to learn more than he could have imagined about the pressures and strains of becoming a parent.

'Funny and moving, *Flour Babies* is an uplifting, self-raising story' – *Guardian*

Winner of the Carnegie Medal and the Whitbread Children's Novel Award

Goggle-Eyes

by Anne Fine

'When it comes to a story, I just tell 'em better.'

Kitty Killin is not only a good story-teller but also the World's Great Expert when it comes to mothers having new and unwanted boyfriends, particularly when there's the danger they might turn into new and unwanted stepfathers.

Funny, touching, with Anne Fine's distinctive blend of humour and realism, this is an irresistible tale.

'*Goggle-Eyes* is a winner: witty, sensitive and warmhearted ... a lovely book' – *Guardian*

Winner of the Carnegie Medal and the *Guardian* Children's Fiction Award

A Pack of Liars

by Anne Fine

Why is it that all the penpals Laura and Oliver get are either so boring they send you to sleep, or complete basket cases? For Laura, tedious Miranda is the last straw. So, taking on the identity of the imaginary Lady Melody Estelle Priscilla Hermione Irwin, Laura begins an extraordinary correspondence with the unsuspecting Miranda and weaves a fantastic tissue of lies about herself and her exotic life. But Laura soon learns she's not the only one capable of successful deception ...

Fast and funny, sharp and perceptive, this is a captivating story by a first-class writer.

'As entertainment it rates highly' – *Junior Bookshelf*

Step by Wicked Step

by Anne Fine

As the lightning flashes and the thunder rolls around the haunted towers of Old Harwick Hall, five stranded schoolchildren uncover the story of Richard Clayton Harwick – a boy who many years ago learned what it was like to have a truly wicked stepfather. But the children have stories of their own step-parents to tell that don't come straight from the dark world of fairy tales – stories that have warmth and humour, as well as sadness, and a fair share of happy endings.

'For children who have some similar experience, this novel will be therapeutic; for those who haven't, it's an absorbing read, to make them laugh and cry' – *Sunday Times*

'Adult readers will surely also enjoy this sunny but riveting book' – *Independent*

CRITICAL ACCLAIM FOR ANNE FINE

About *Step by Wicked Step* . . .

'This author can make you laugh and cry and is
too much of a treasure to be reserved for
children alone'
– Nicholas Tucker, *Independent*

'In writing so clearly without losing human
depth, Anne Fine proves herself once again to
be a children's writer of rare gifts'
– David Buckley, *The Times Educational
Supplement*

. . . about *Flour Babies* . . .

'*Flour Babies* shines out like a beacon. A
beautifully crafted book, very funny, and often
moving, yet completely unsentimental'
– Sara O'Reilly, *Time Out*

. . . and *Goggle-Eyes* . . .

'A refreshingly funny book with a sensible base
. . . whoever fails to laugh must have a heart of
cement' – Naomi Lewis, *Observer*

READ MORE IN PUFFIN

For children of all ages, Puffin represents quality and variety – the very best in publishing today around the world.

For complete information about books available from Puffin – and Penguin – and how to order them, contact us at the appropriate address below. Please note that for copyright reasons the selection of books varies from country to country.

On the worldwide web: www.puffin.co.uk

In the United Kingdom: Please write to *Dept. EP, Penguin Books Ltd, Bath Road, Harmondsworth, West Drayton, Middlesex UB7 ODA*
Schools Line in the UK: Please write to

In the United States: Please write to *Consumer Sales, Penguin USA, P.O. Box 999, Dept. 17109, Bergenfield, New Jersey 07621-0120.* VISA and MasterCard holders call 1-800-253-6476 to order Penguin titles

In Canada: Please write to *Penguin Books Canada Ltd, 10 Alcorn Avenue, Suite 300, Toronto, Ontario M4V 3B2*

In Australia: Please write to *Penguin Books Australia Ltd, P.O. Box 257, Ringwood, Victoria 3134*

In New Zealand: Please write to *Penguin Books (NZ) Ltd, Private Bag 102902, North Shore Mail Centre, Auckland 10*

In India: Please write to *Penguin Books India Pvt Ltd, 706 Eros Apartments, 56 Nehru Place, New Delhi 110 019*

In the Netherlands: Please write to *Penguin Books Netherlands bv, Postbus 3507, NL-1001 AH Amsterdam*

In Germany: Please write to *Penguin Books Deutschland GmbH, Metzlerstrasse 26, 60594 Frankfurt am Main*

In Spain: Please write to *Penguin Books S. A., Bravo Murillo 19, 1° B, 28015 Madrid*

In Italy: Please write to *Penguin Italia s.r.l., Via Felice Casati 20, I-20124 Milano*

In France: Please write to *Penguin France S. A., 17 rue Lejeune, F-31000 Toulouse*

In Japan: Please write to *Penguin Books Japan, Ishikiribashi Building, 2-5-4, Suido, Bunkyo-ku, Tokyo 112*

In South Africa: Please write to *Longman Penguin Southern Africa (Pty) Ltd, Private Bag X08, Bertsham 2013*